Noddy's Perfect Gift

HarperCollins *Children's Books*

It was a peaceful morning in Toy Town, until…

VROOM! Noddy's little yellow car roared up the road and screeched to a halt outside Toadstool House.

   Noddy jumped out, pushed open the front door and dashed inside.

   "Big-Ears! Big-Ears!" he shouted.

"It must be very important if you're in such a rush, Noddy," said Big-Ears. "What's the problem?"

"I don't know! I don't know! I don't know!" cried Noddy, pacing up and down.

"Well, if *you* don't know what the problem is, how can I possibly help you?" said Big-Ears.

Noddy tried to explain.

"Oh, Big-Ears, I'm not sure if my birthday present for Tessie Bear is enough. It's just a song I made up."

"A song sounds like a lovely present, Noddy," said Big-Ears smiling. "Sing it and I'll tell you what I think."

Noddy cleared his throat and began to sing:
> *This song is for your birthday, Tessie Bear, it's true.*
> *Yes, every note I've written is especially for you.*
> *I like you, Tessie Bear, you must know it's true.*
> *Friend of mine, every line shows how much I do.*

"What do you think, Big-Ears?" Noddy asked.
"Should it be longer? Shorter? Prettier?"
"It's perfect just as it is, Noddy," said Big-Ears.
"Are you sure, Big-Ears?" said Noddy.
"She'll love it, Noddy," Big-Ears promised him.
"Off you go, now! And don't come back until
you've sung it to her."

Noddy set off to see Tessie Bear.

   Suddenly someone called out, "Taxi! Taxi!"
It was Martha Monkey. Noddy pulled over.

   "Sorry Martha, I can't give you a lift, I've
got something very important to do!"

   But Martha just jumped in. "Oh, please,
Noddy, I need to get to Town Square."

   "OK then," sighed Noddy.

"I hear it's Tessie Bear's birthday," said Martha, when they arrived in Toy Town. "Is she having a party? Who's invited? And, most important, what are you giving her?"

"A song! I made it up myself," said Noddy.

"A song is nice, I suppose," said Martha, "but it might not be enough to make her feel *extra* special."

Noddy looked worried again. Perhaps a song wasn't the best present, after all.

"Oh, Martha," he cried. "What *would* make Tessie Bear feel extra special?"

"Flowers always make *me* feel special," said Martha giving him a wink.

"Of course! Flowers!" Noddy whooped happily. "Why didn't I think of that?"

Noddy was sure Tessie Bear would like the
forget-me-nots he'd bought. They were just
like the flowers on her hat.

"What lovely flowers," said Mr Wobbly Man.

"They're for Tessie Bear," Noddy told him
proudly. "And I've made up a special birthday
song for her."

"Lucky Tessie!" said Mr Wobbly Man. "But what about a cake? A cake is the best part of a birthday."

"Oh, no! I didn't think of that," wailed Noddy. "I've just got time to make one. Will you help me?"

Whirrrrrrrr… went the mixing machine.

"Phew! Whipping up a cake is hard work," said Noddy.

"Let me taste it for you," said Mr Wobbly Man, scooping some of the creamy mixture into his mouth.

"Hmmm. This cake mixture needs a little more… tasting!" said Mr Wobbly Man and he gobbled it all up!

"Sorry, Noddy, you'll have to make another one,"
said Mr Wobbly Man.

"But I've only got enough eggs for a bite-sized
cake, this time," moaned Noddy. "No more tasting,
Mr Wobbly Man!" he said firmly, measuring more
flour into his mixing bowl.

"Small but perfect," said Noddy proudly as
he took the cake out of the oven. "And it smells
scrumptious."

"Shall I have a little taste, just to make sure?"
suggested Mr Wobbly Man.

"No!" cried Noddy, snatching the cake away.
"I'm taking it to Tessie Bear, right now!"

But Mr Wobbly Man started to groan. "Ooo, my tummy! I've eaten too much cake mixture."

Poor Noddy had to drive Mr Wobbly Man to the shop to get some medicine. Would he ever get to Tessie Bear's house?

As he came out of the shop, Noddy saw Sly and Gobbo, the two goblins, leaning over his car.

"Hey!" Noddy shouted. "What are you up to?"

The naughty goblins jumped back.

"We were, er... you tell him, Sly," said Gobbo.

"Me?" said Sly. "Oh, OK. We were trying to snatch –"

SLAP! Gobbo slapped a hand over Sly's mouth and hissed, "*Sniff* not *snatch*. We were just sniffing the pretty flowers. The cake smelt yummy, too."

Noddy rushed to his car. The cake and flowers
were safe. "Those are my presents for Tessie's
birthday," he told the goblins.

"Birthday presents, eh?" said Gobbo thoughtfully.
"We can help with presents, can't we, Sly?"

And he yanked Sly aside to whisper to him.
There was a lot of giggling and Sly kept nodding
his head.

Finally, the two cheeky goblins turned back to Noddy. Gobbo said, "Sly and I think the best way to make Tessie Bear happy is to give her…"

"…some jelly!" sniggered Sly.

"No!" hissed Gobbo. "Jewellery!"

"Jewellery?" said Noddy, looking worried.

"Yes and we know where you can get it," said Gobbo.

"Step this way for some wonderful jewellery,"
said Gobbo, hurrying Noddy down a back street.

"Are you sure there's a jewellery shop here?"
said Noddy, wondering if he should trust them.

"Oh, yes," said Sly. "Look!"

"What? Where? In these boxes?" gasped Noddy.

"This box is full of jewellery," said Gobbo, trying not to giggle. "Look! You'll be surprised."

Noddy thought it might be a trick but he just couldn't help peeping into the box.

Quick as a flash, Sly and Gobbo pushed him in and shut the lid. Poor Noddy was trapped!

"Yep! He was surprised, all right," chortled Sly.

"Now for the great car snatch!" yelled Gobbo.

The goblins raced down the street and dived
into Noddy's car. Shrieking with laughter, they
roared up and down the road, beeping the horn.

PARP! PARP!

And, to tease poor Noddy, they gave an extra
loud beep every time they passed.

THUNK. THUNK. THUNK. The box bumped angrily down the street.

Then, just as Mr Plod walked by, the box suddenly jumped!

"Aghh!" the policeman shouted in surprise.

A loud knocking came from inside the box. Mr Plod crept closer to have a look.

All at once, the box burst open and up popped Noddy! He was very cross.

"Arrest them, Mr Plod," he cried. "They're stealing my car!"

"Who? What? Where?" gasped Mr Plod, looking all around.

Just then, the goblins came roaring down
the road in Noddy's little car.

"Why, those scoundrels!" said Mr Plod.
He stepped into the road, raised his hand
and blew a loud blast on his whistle.

"PEEEEP! Stop in the name of Plod!"
he commanded.

Gobbo braked hard. The little yellow car screeched to a halt, only just missing Mr Plod.

The two goblins bashed their noses on the windscreen. "Aghh! Ouch!" they groaned.

"You ought to be ashamed of yourselves, stealing Noddy's car like that," Mr Plod told them sternly.

"Sorry, Mr Plod," said Gobbo. "Sometimes our naughty side just runs away with us!"

"Yeah, like now!" yelled Sly. And the two naughty goblins leaped out of the car and ran away, hooting with laughter. Mr Plod raced off after them, blowing his whistle. PEEEP-PEEP!

Poor Noddy. His cake and flowers were crushed to bits.

"What's the matter, Noddy?" asked Big-Ears,
who was passing by.

"I wanted to give Tessie an *extra*-special birthday.
But Sly and Gobbo have wrecked everything,"
cried Noddy.

"But what about your song? It came straight
from your heart," said Big-Ears. "It's a perfect
present!"

"You really think so?" said Noddy. And he
rushed off to find Tessie.

This song is for your birthday, Tessie Bear, it's true.
Yes, every note I've written is especially for you.
I like you, Tessie Bear, you must know it's true.
Friend of mine, every line shows how much I do.
Noddy stopped singing and looked shyly at Tessie.
"Thank you, Noddy!" She beamed at him.
"It's the most perfect present I've ever had!"

This edition produced for The Book People Ltd,
Hall Wood Avenue, Haydock, St Helens, WA11 9UL
First published in Great Britain by HarperCollins Publishers Ltd in 2002

1

This edition published by HarperCollins Children's Books
HarperCollins Children's Books is a division of HarperCollins Publishers Ltd.

Text and images copyright © 2002 Enid Blyton Ltd (a Chorion company).
The word "NODDY" is a registered trade mark of Enid Blyton Ltd. All rights reserved.
For further information on Noddy please contact www.NODDY.com

ISBN: 978 0 00 783071 8

Visit our website at: www.harpercollinschildrensbooks.co.uk

Printed and bound by South China Printing Co. Ltd